MR. STRONG

looks for a job

Roger Hargreaves

Original concept by Roger Hargreaves
Illustrated and written by Adam Hargreaves

MR. MEN   **LITTLE MISS**

MR. MEN™ LITTLE MISS™ © THOIP (a SANRIO company)

Mr Strong Looks for a Job © 2014 THOIP (a SANRIO company)
Printed and published under licence from Penguin Random House LLC
This edition published in 2019 by Dean, an imprint of Egmont UK Limited,
The Yellow Building, 1 Nicholas Road, London W11 4AN

ISBN 978 0 6035 7125 1
61261/001
Printed in Great Britain

Egmont takes its responsibility to the planet and its inhabitants very seriously.
We aim to use paper from well-managed forests run by responsible suppliers.

DEAN

Mr Strong was the strongest person you've ever met. But he had a problem. He was too strong for any job.

If he washed a car, all the paint would rub off.

If he painted a house, the house would fall down.

He was much too strong.

But that morning, Mr Strong had at last found a job that sounded just right for him …

Zoo keeper!

And he could start the next week.

On Monday, Mr Strong was put in charge of cleaning the monkey cage.

He scrubbed and rubbed and brushed and brushed some more.

Hee hee! The monkeys giggled as they watched him work.

But he brushed so hard that … SNAP! The handle of the brush broke!

"Whoops," said Mr Strong.

Hee hee hee! The monkeys laughed more than ever.

On Tuesday, Mr Strong was put in charge of feeding the penguins.

He drove the tractor straight into the water.

"Sorry!" called Mr Strong to the surprised penguins.

On Wednesday, Mr Strong was put in charge of the panda.

Do you think he used the door to get into the cage?

Not at all! He stretched the bars of the cage and simply walked straight in. Easy!

But, seeing his chance, the panda ran towards the gap in the bars and, with a big smile on his face, he escaped!

"Sorry!" said Mr Strong.

On Thursday, Mr Strong was not put in charge of any animals.

He was put in charge of selling ice creams.

What could possibly go wrong?

Ice cream cornets are small. And ice cream cornets are not very strong.

Whoops!

"I'm so sorry," said Mr Strong to his sticky customers.

On Friday, Mr Strong was put in charge of the washing up.

But the plates didn't last for long.

CRASH!

"Oh dear, I can't do anything right," said Mr Strong.

Without a doubt Mr Strong was just too strong.

Perhaps the zoo wasn't the place for him …

But on Saturday, Mr Strong was given a job that, for once, really used his strength.

Lifting the baby elephant into his bath!

Like all babies, the elephant loved taking a bath and he even had a rubber duck to play with!

The head zoo keeper was delighted.

"Well done, Mr Strong. This job is perfect for you. I have an idea …"

Now Mr Strong comes to the zoo every Saturday to bath the baby elephant and sometimes even the mummy and daddy elephants …

But juggling the elephants is strictly forbidden!